AUTO-B-GOOD™

EJ AND THE BULLY

A LESSON IN RESPECT

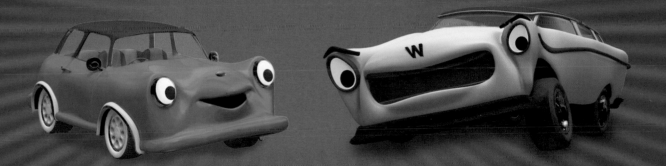

WRITTEN BY **PHILLIP WALTON**

ART BY **RISING STAR STUDIOS**

Free Activities, Coloring Pages, and Character Building Lessons Available Online!
www.risingstareducation.com

RISINGSTAR
S T U D I O S

EJ AND THE BULLY: A Lesson in Respect

Written by Phillip Walton

A story based on the characters from the series Auto-B-Good™

ART & EDITORIAL DIRECTOR
Tom Oswald

CONTRIBUTING EDITOR
Nick Rogosienski

ADDITIONAL EDITING
Colleen Sexton

LEAD 3D ARTIST
Phillip Walton

ADDITIONAL ART
Drew Blom
Bruce Pukema

GRAPHIC DESIGNER AND LETTERER
Steve Plummer

COVER DESIGN
Steve Plummer

PRODUCTION MANAGER
Nick Rogosienski

PRODUCTION COORDINATOR
Mark Nordling

SPECIAL THANKS
John Richards
Linda Bettes
Barbara Gruener
Jack Currier

Printed in China:
Shenzhen Donnelley Printing Co., Ltd
Shenzhen, Guangdong Province, China
Completed: February 2010
P1_0210

Publisher's Cataloging-In-Publication Data
(Prepared by The Donohue Group, Inc.)

Walton, Phillip.
  EJ and the bully : a lesson in respect / written by Phillip Walton ; art by Rising Star Studios.
    p. : ill. (holographic) ; cm. -- (Auto-B-Good)

  Previously published in 2009.
  Summary: A story based on the characters from the video series Auto-B-Good. When EJ is bullied at school, his friend Derek helps EJ realize he is valuable and worthy of respect.
  Interest age level: 005-009.
  ISBN: 978-1-936086-42-9 (hardcover/library binding)
  ISBN: 978-1-936086-48-1 (pbk.)

1. Respect--Juvenile fiction. 2. Self-esteem--Juvenile fiction. 3. Bullies--Juvenile fiction. 4. Respect--Fiction. 5. Self-esteem--Fiction. 6. Bullies--Fiction. I. Rising Star Studios. II. Title.

PZ7.W3586 Ej 2010
[E]

2009913117

VOTE FOR CLASS PRESIDENT

"EJ for class president!" EJ called as he handed out flyers to students.

Suddenly, Izzi rushed up beside him. "EJ! Someone tore down your campaign posters."

"What?" EJ yelped. "Why would someone do that?"

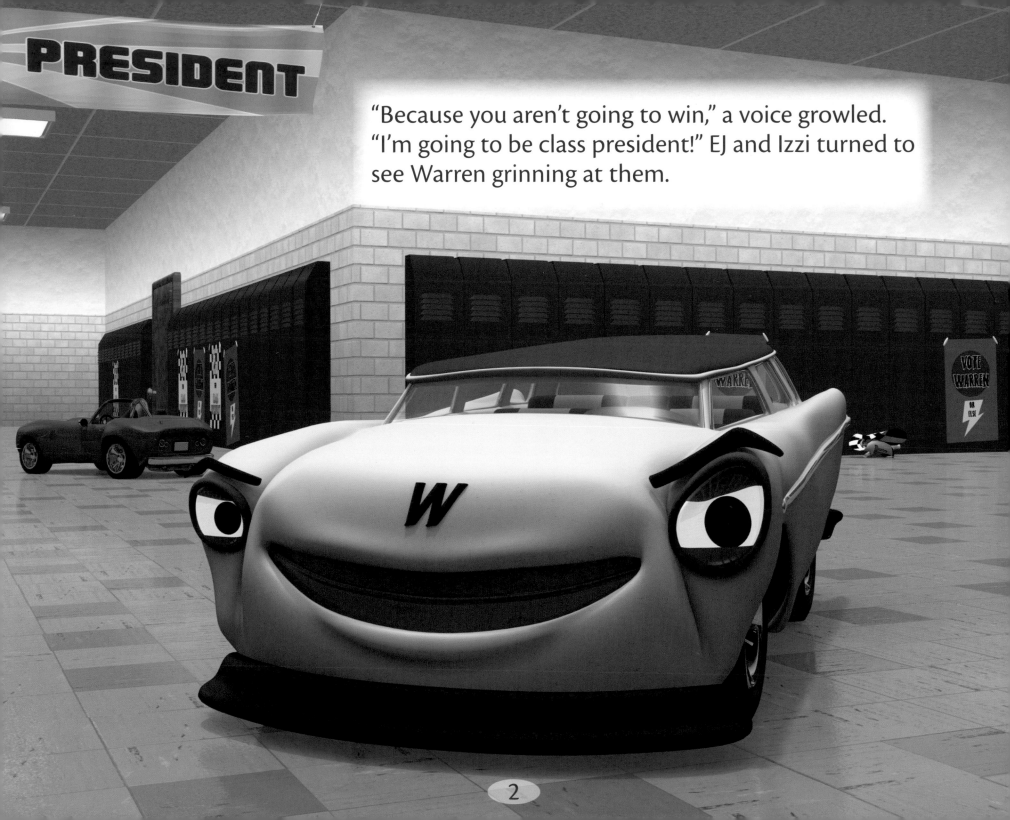

"Because you aren't going to win," a voice growled. "I'm going to be class president!" EJ and Izzi turned to see Warren grinning at them.

"He's only running against me because I promised I would stop his bullying," EJ said after Warren left.

"I hope he doesn't win," Izzi said. "Warren is mean and rude."

"Do you need help putting your posters back up?" Izzi asked.

"Nah, I got it," EJ said. "It'll take more than that to get me to quit."

5

EJ was taping up a poster in the back hallway. Suddenly, mud splashed all over him. EJ was covered!

EJ rounded the corner and came face to face with Warren. He was already laughing. Other cars saw EJ and began to laugh, too.

Mr. Wheeler rushed over to help. "What's going on!" the teacher exclaimed.

Warren laughed. "I guess EJ is just another dirty politician! **VOTE FOR WARREN!**"

EJ was so embarrassed.
He raced out of school
and headed for home.

On the way home, EJ saw Derek. "Hey, EJ. How is the campaign?" Derek asked. "Looks like there's been some political mudslinging!"

"Real funny Derek," EJ grumbled.

"Warren dumped mud on me in front of everyone," EJ said. "Now nobody will take me seriously. I'll never be class president. I'm just going to quit."

"Got a bully after you, huh?" Derek said. "Come on. Let's go get you cleaned up."

They stopped at EJ's house and hauled out a garden hose. "Don't bother," EJ said sadly. "Leave the mud on. I deserve it. I never should have tried to stand up to Warren. Everyone respects him, but no one respects me."

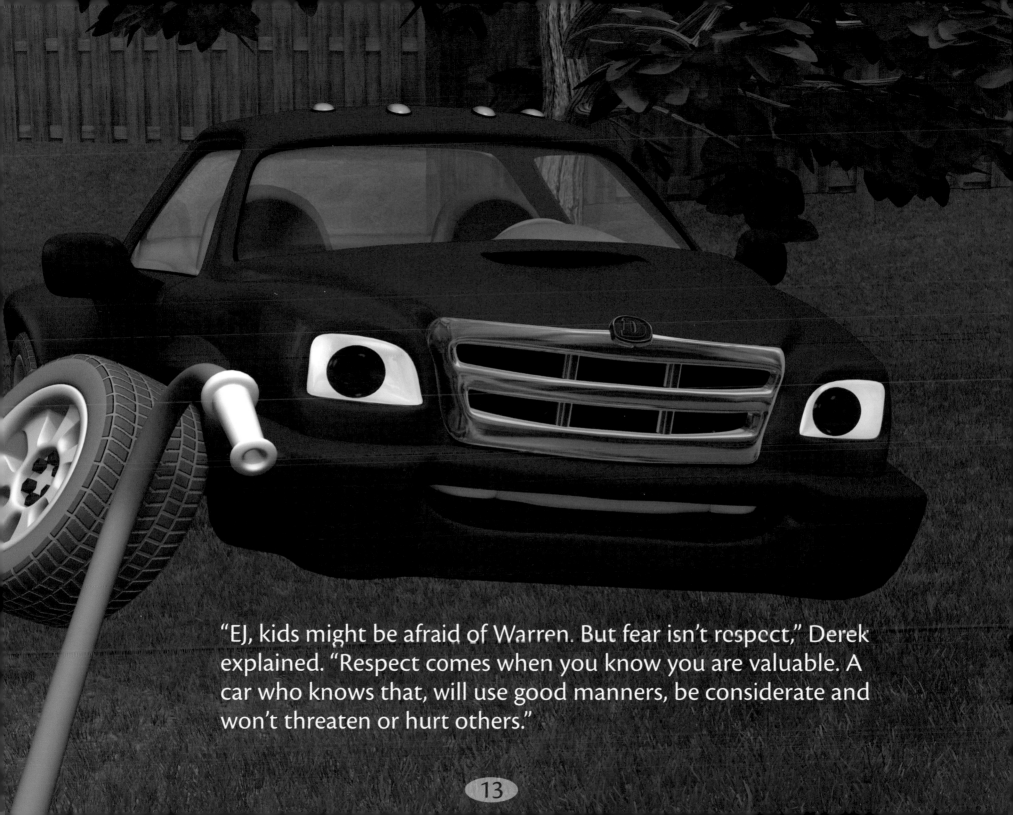

"EJ, kids might be afraid of Warren. But fear isn't respect," Derek explained. "Respect comes when you know you are valuable. A car who knows that, will use good manners, be considerate and won't threaten or hurt others."

"How do I know if I'm valuable?" EJ asked.

14

"EJ, even under all that mud, you are still a valuable car made with the finest quality craftsmanship," Derek said.

He grabbed the hose and began to spray the mud off EJ.

"BRR! Derek!" EJ shouted as the cold water splashed him.

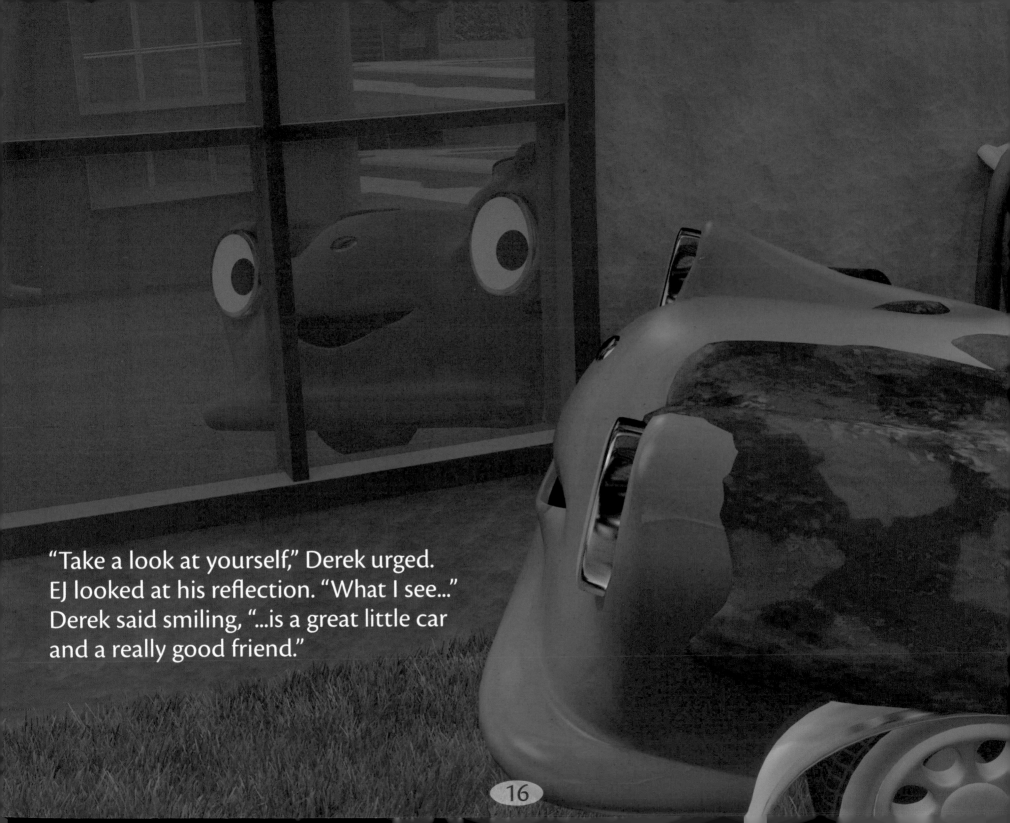

"Take a look at yourself," Derek urged. EJ looked at his reflection. "What I see..." Derek said smiling, "...is a great little car and a really good friend."

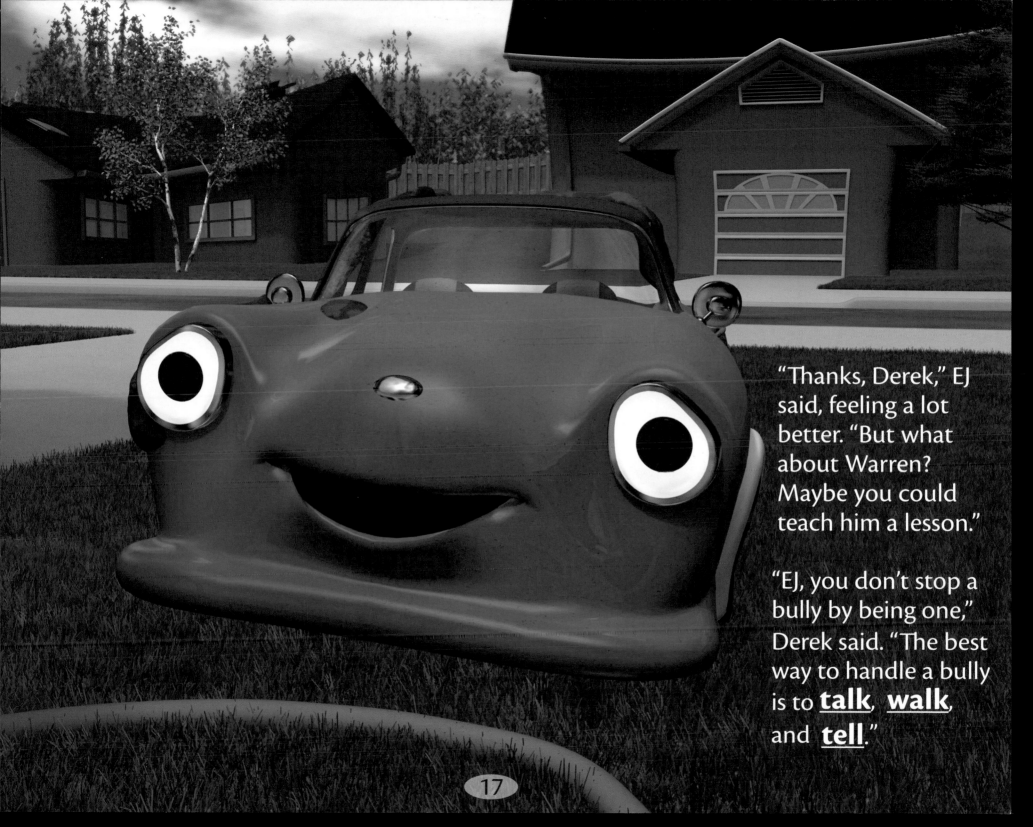

"Thanks, Derek," EJ said, feeling a lot better. "But what about Warren? Maybe you could teach him a lesson."

"EJ, you don't stop a bully by being one," Derek said. "The best way to handle a bully is to **talk**, **walk**, and **tell**."

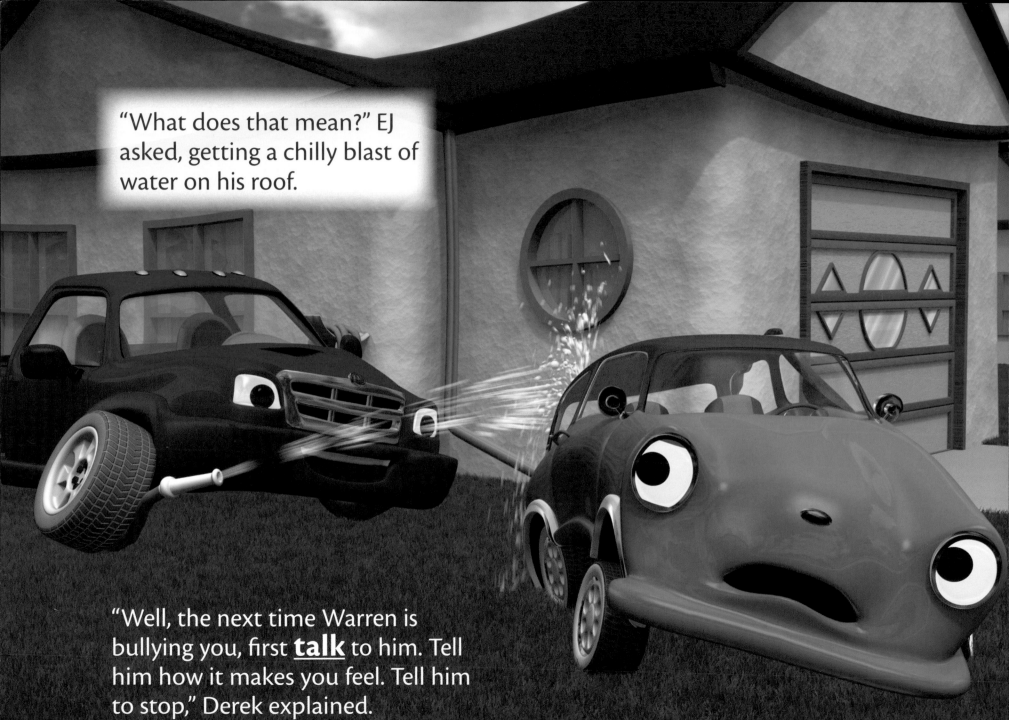

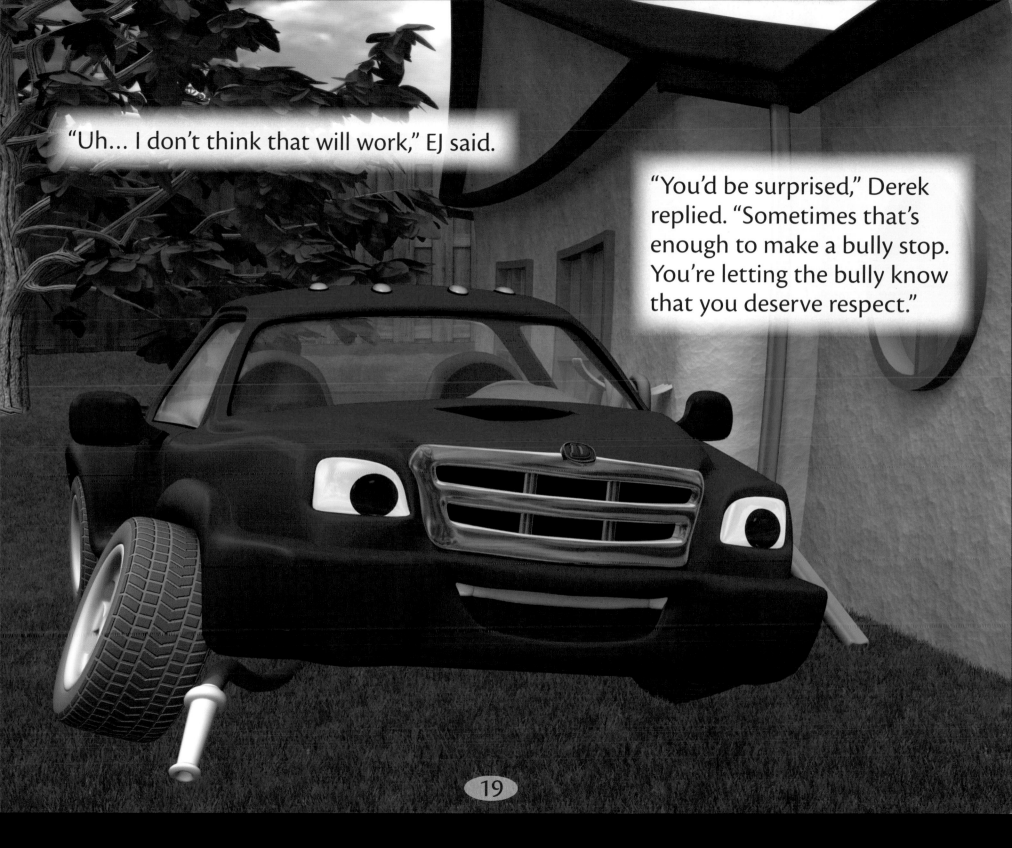

"Uh… I don't think that will work," EJ said.

"You'd be surprised," Derek replied. "Sometimes that's enough to make a bully stop. You're letting the bully know that you deserve respect."

"But what if Warren keeps bullying me?" EJ asked.

Derek sprayed the last bit of mud from EJ's fender. "Then you **walk**, EJ. Don't fight and argue. A bully wants you to get upset. So it's best to leave before things get out of hand."

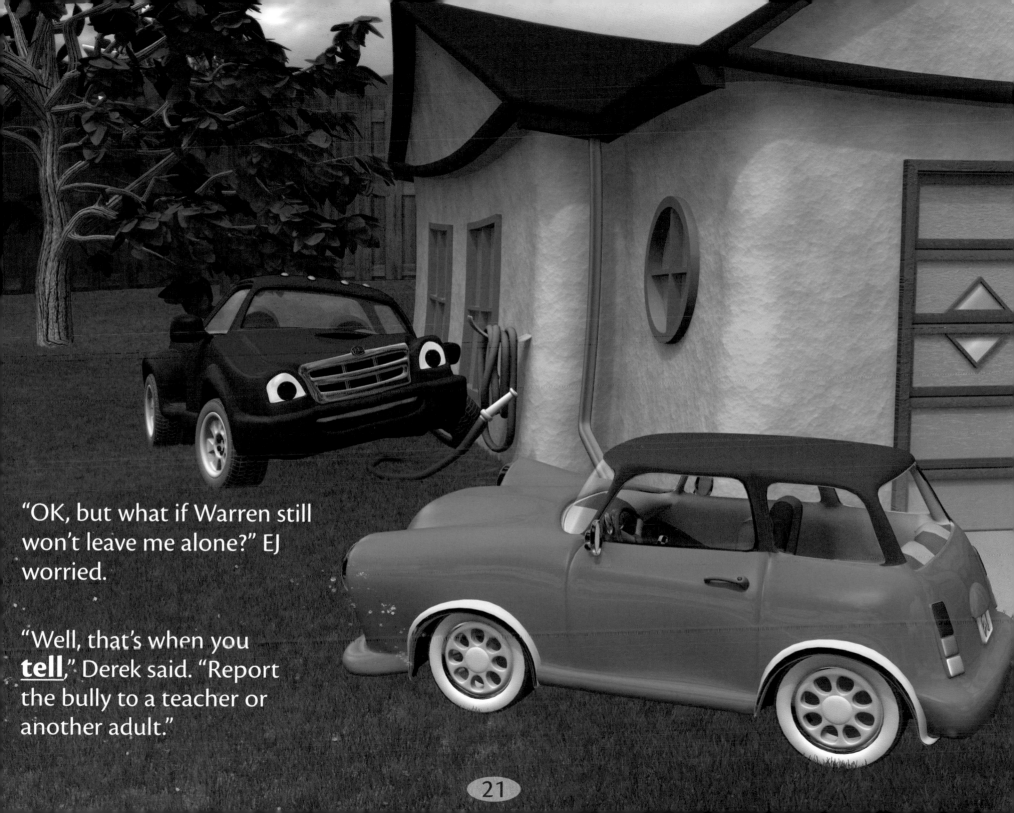

"OK, but what if Warren still won't leave me alone?" EJ worried.

"Well, that's when you **tell**," Derek said. "Report the bully to a teacher or another adult."

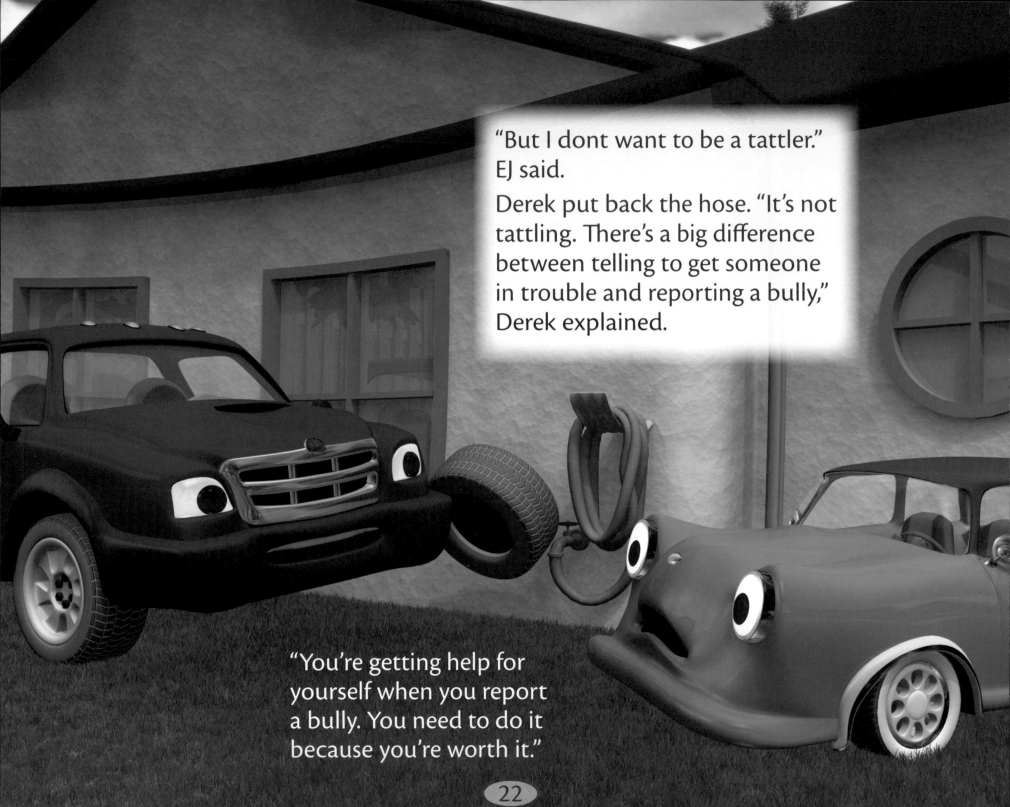

"But I dont want to be a tattler." EJ said.

Derek put back the hose. "It's not tattling. There's a big difference between telling to get someone in trouble and reporting a bully," Derek explained.

"You're getting help for yourself when you report a bully. You need to do it because you're worth it."

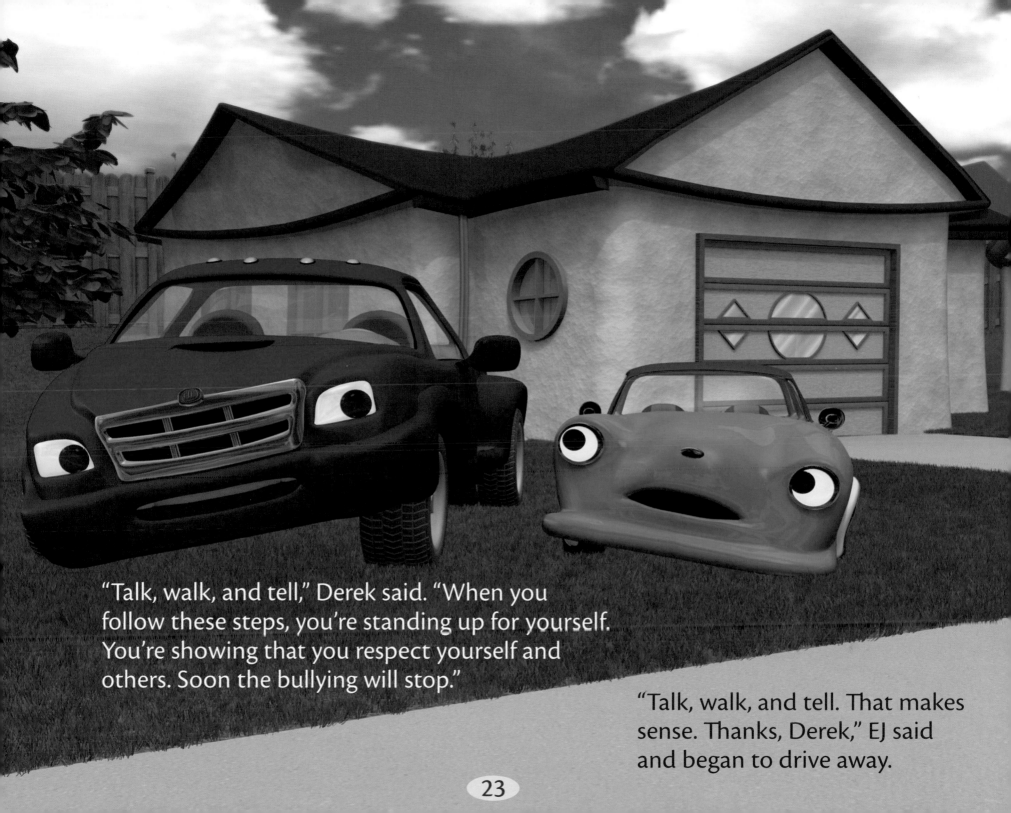

"Talk, walk, and tell," Derek said. "When you follow these steps, you're standing up for yourself. You're showing that you respect yourself and others. Soon the bullying will stop."

"Talk, walk, and tell. That makes sense. Thanks, Derek," EJ said and began to drive away.

"Where are you going?"
Derek asked.

"Back to school," EJ smiled.
"I've got an election to win."

"Hey, that's the spirit...
Mr. Class President,"
Derek winked.

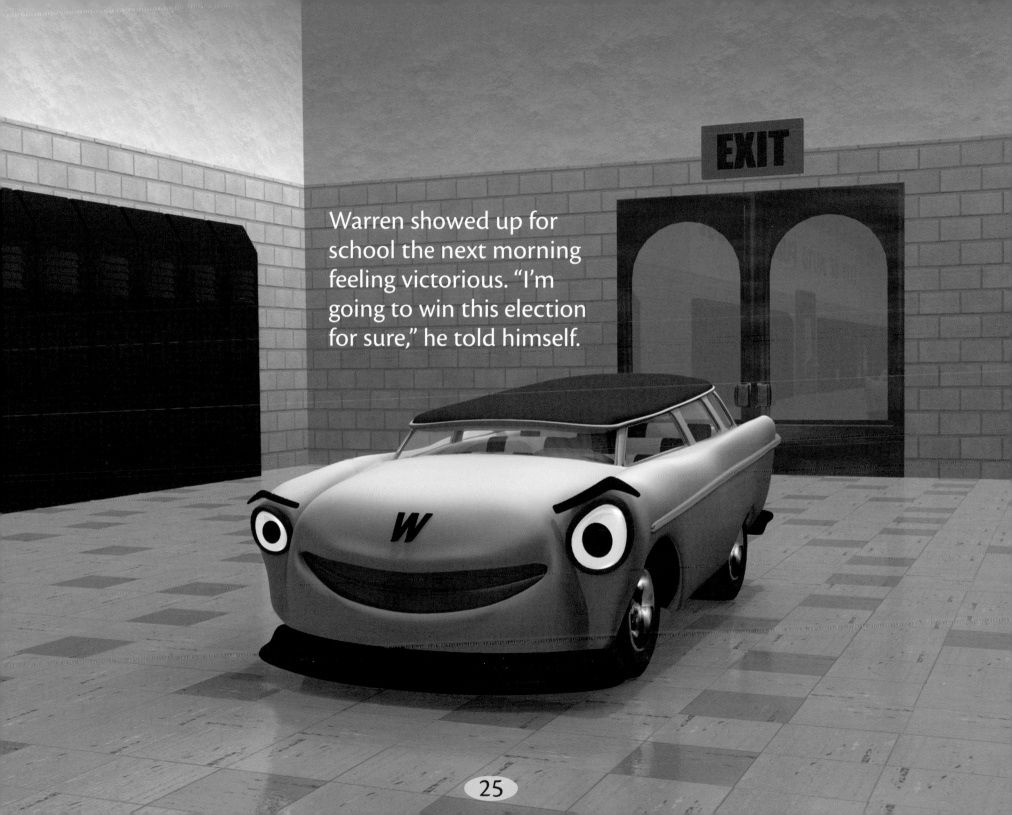

Warren showed up for school the next morning feeling victorious. "I'm going to win this election for sure," he told himself.

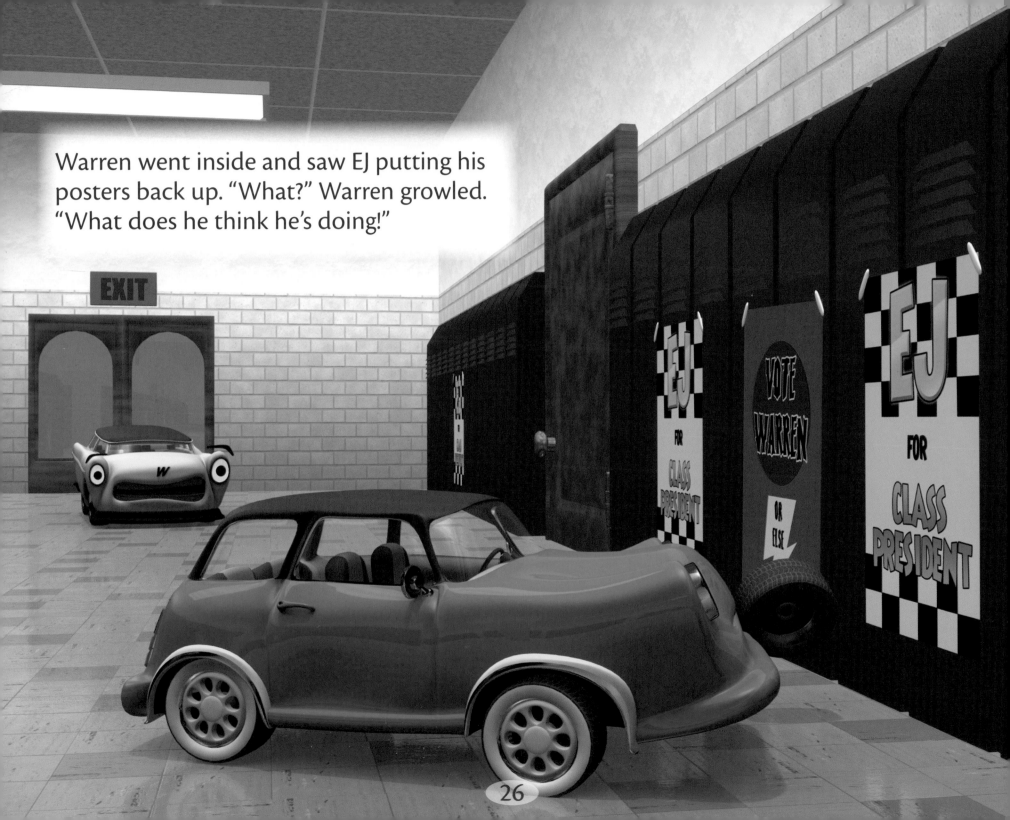

Warren went inside and saw EJ putting his posters back up. "What?" Warren growled. "What does he think he's doing!"

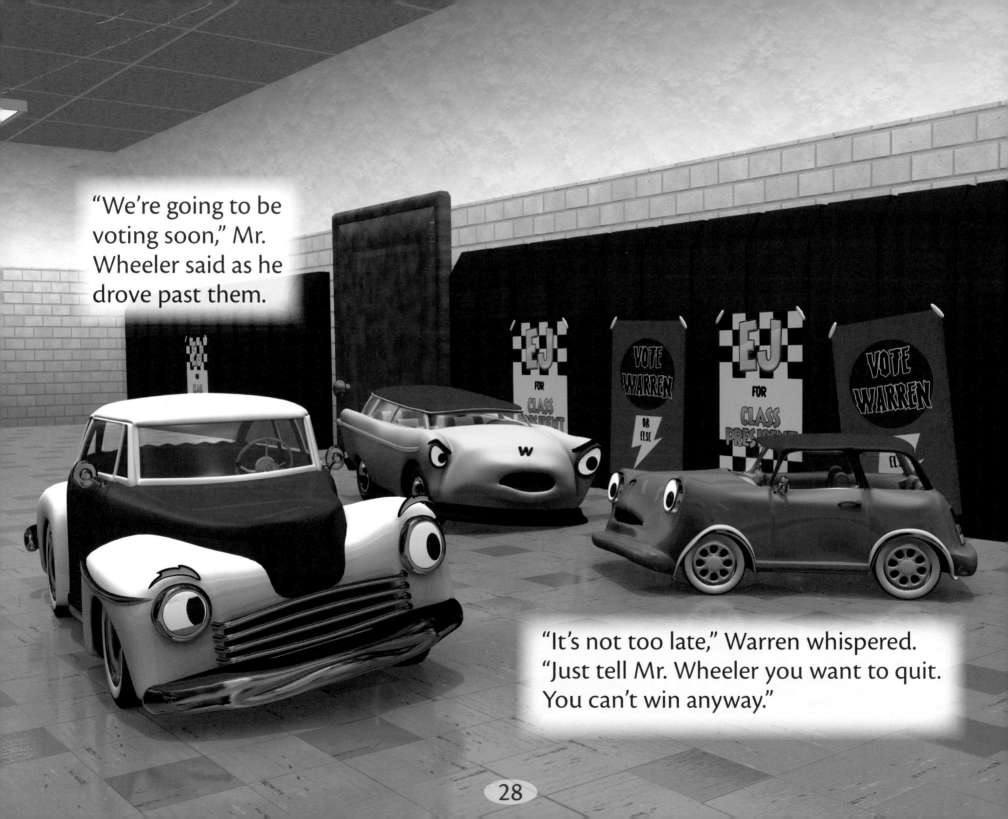

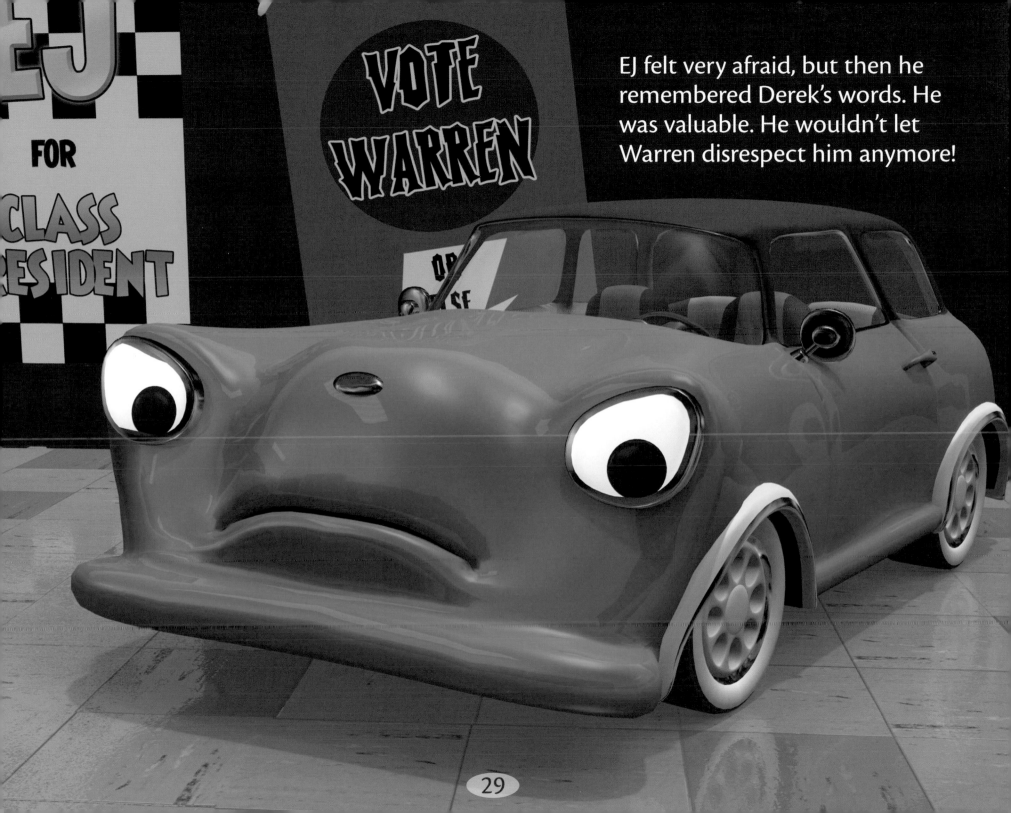

EJ felt very afraid, but then he remembered Derek's words. He was valuable. He wouldn't let Warren disrespect him anymore!

"Warren, I don't like it when you're mean and threaten me. I want you to stop," EJ said.

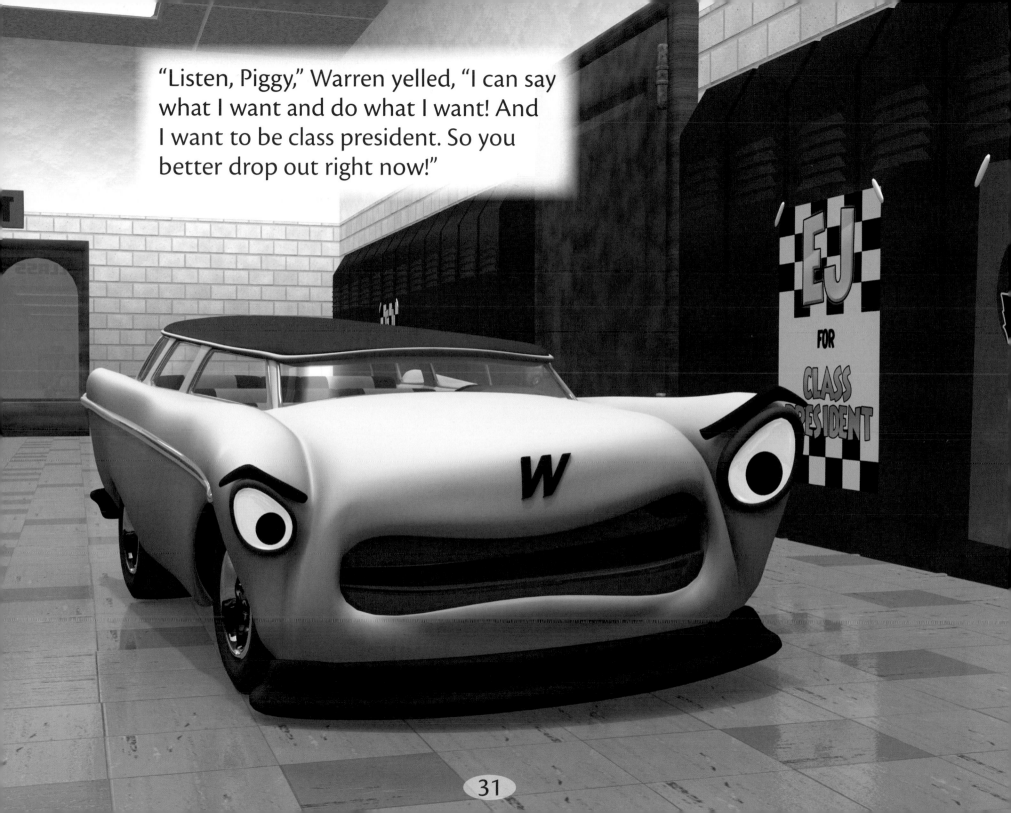

"Listen, Piggy," Warren yelled, "I can say what I want and do what I want! And I want to be class president. So you better drop out right now!"

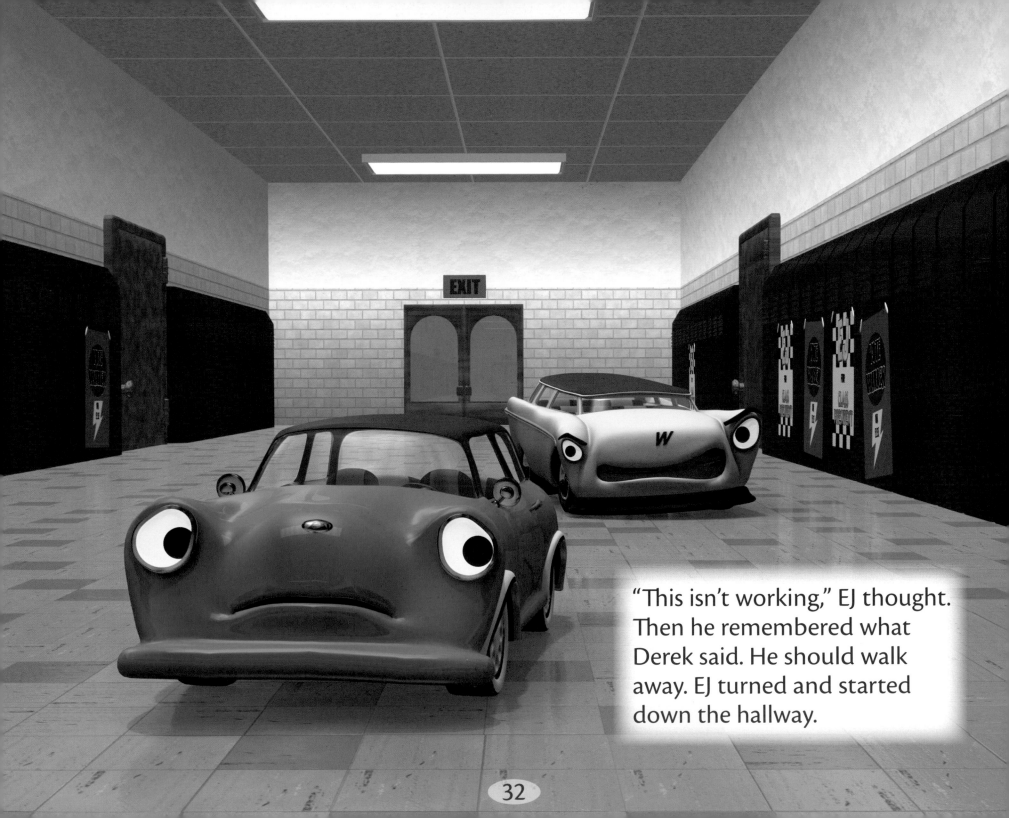

"This isn't working," EJ thought. Then he remembered what Derek said. He should walk away. EJ turned and started down the hallway.

Warren was furious. He zoomed in front of EJ. "You'd better go tell Mr. Wheeler you quit right now… or else," Warren threatened.

EJ panicked. He realized that Warren wasn't going to let him go. "Talk, walk… and tell," EJ thought. He knew what he had to do. "All right, Warren. I guess I have no choice," EJ said. "I'll tell Mr. Wheeler."

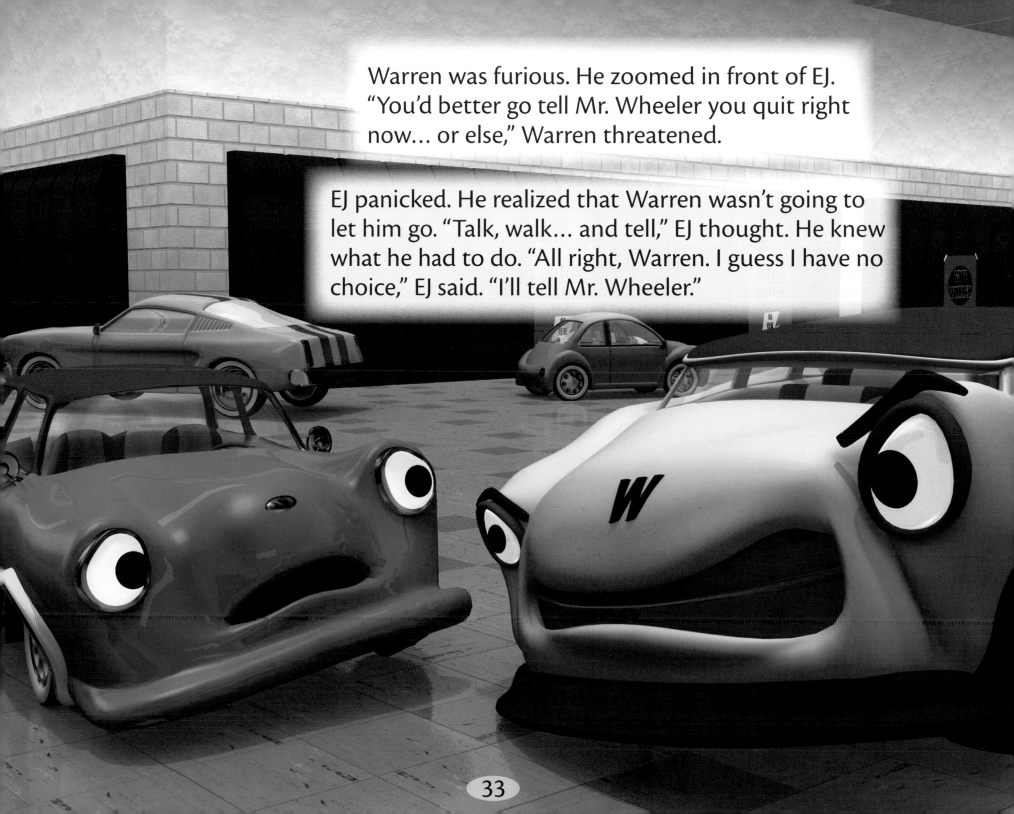

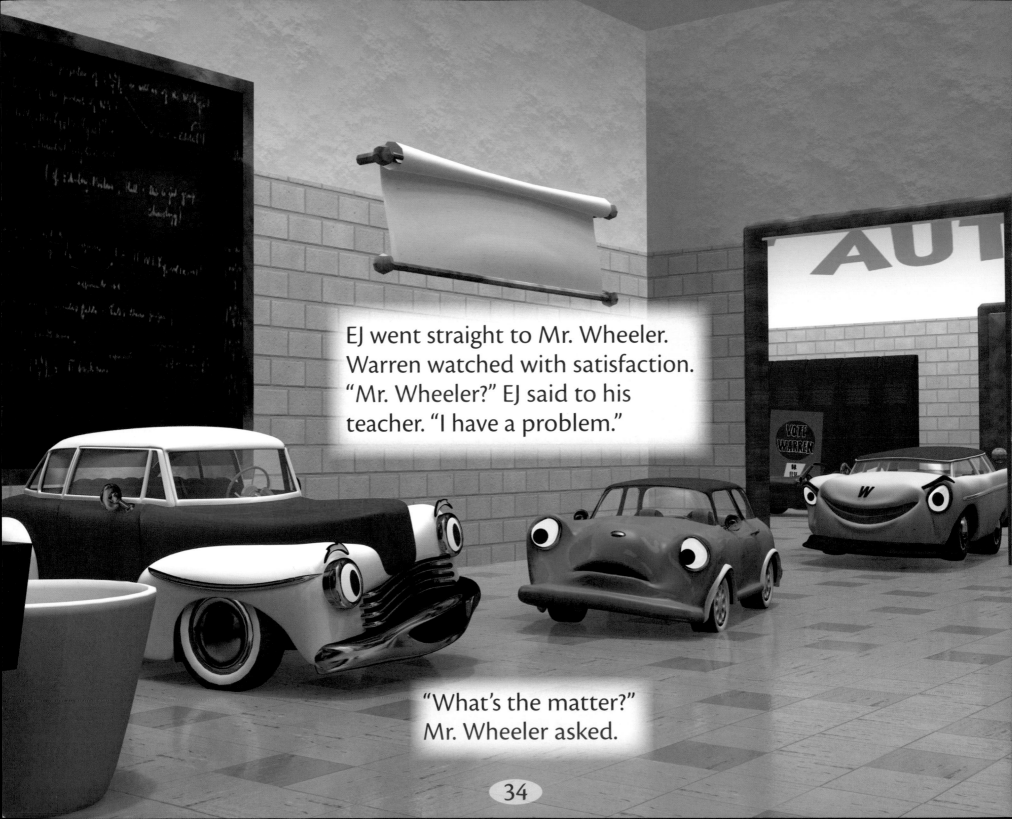

EJ went straight to Mr. Wheeler. Warren watched with satisfaction. "Mr. Wheeler?" EJ said to his teacher. "I have a problem."

"What's the matter?" Mr. Wheeler asked.

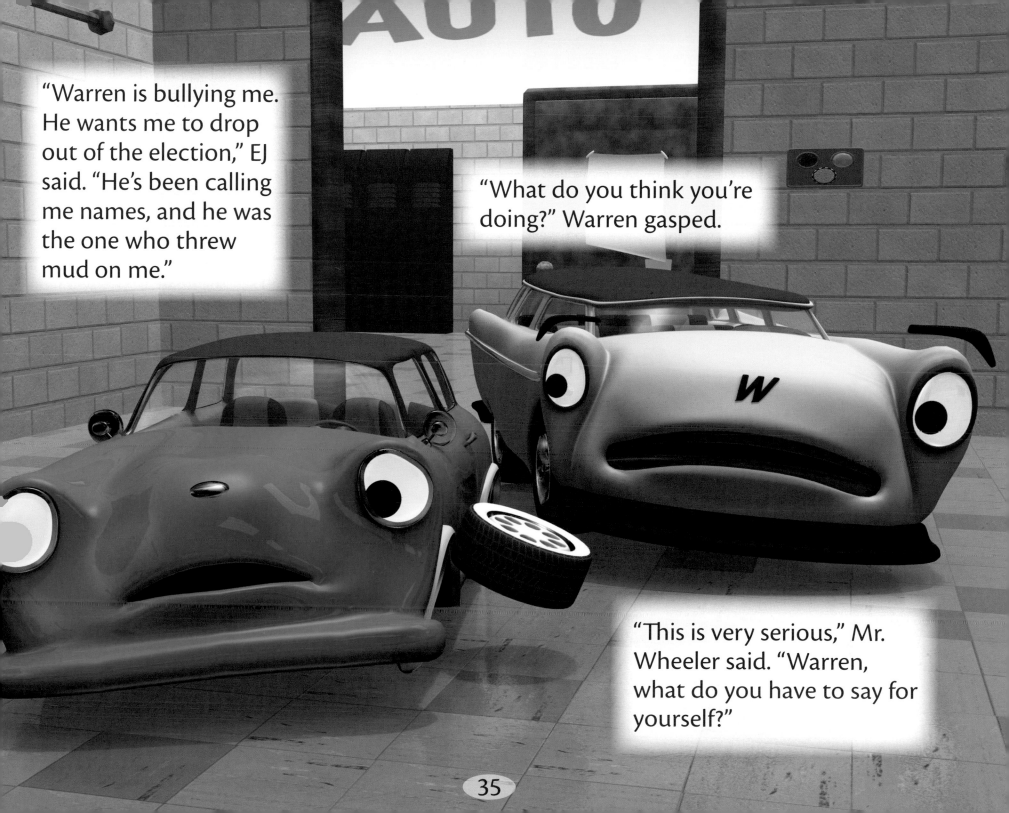

"Warren is bullying me. He wants me to drop out of the election," EJ said. "He's been calling me names, and he was the one who threw mud on me."

"What do you think you're doing?" Warren gasped.

"This is very serious," Mr. Wheeler said. "Warren, what do you have to say for yourself?"

"EJ just can't take a joke," Warren said glaring at EJ.

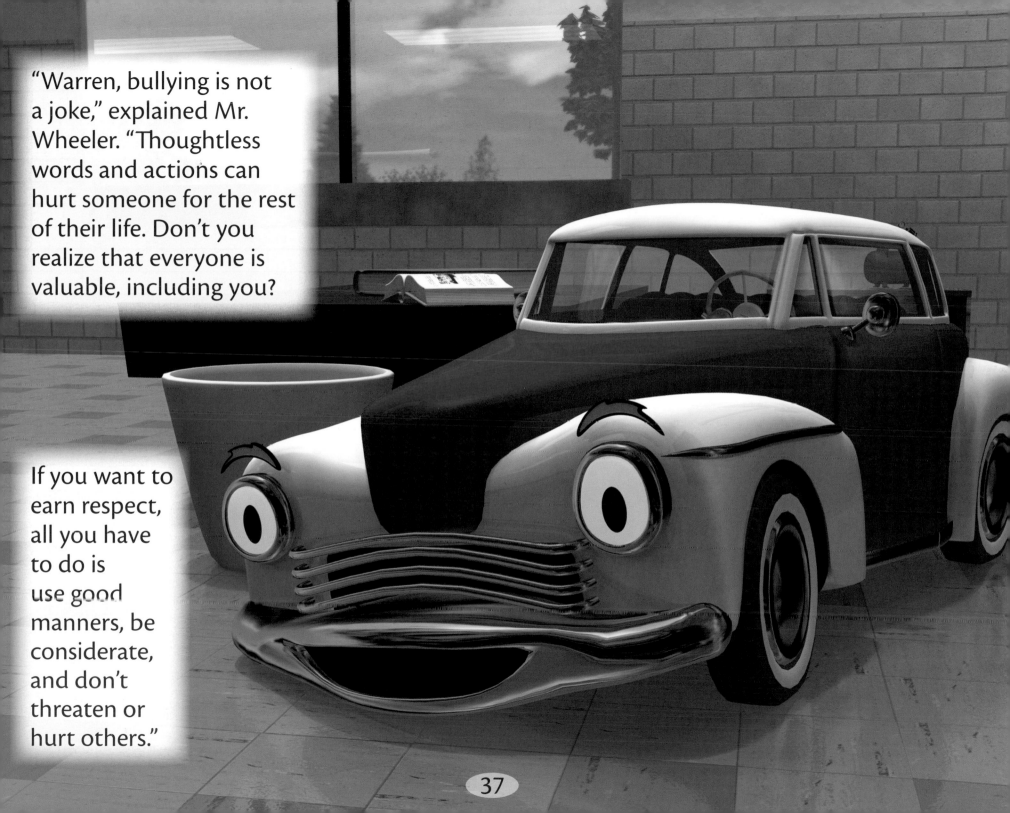

"Warren, bullying is not a joke," explained Mr. Wheeler. "Thoughtless words and actions can hurt someone for the rest of their life. Don't you realize that everyone is valuable, including you?

If you want to earn respect, all you have to do is use good manners, be considerate, and don't threaten or hurt others."

"I like my way better," Warren smirked.

"Really? Well, there will be consequences for your actions," Mr. Wheeler said. "But first, it's time to vote."

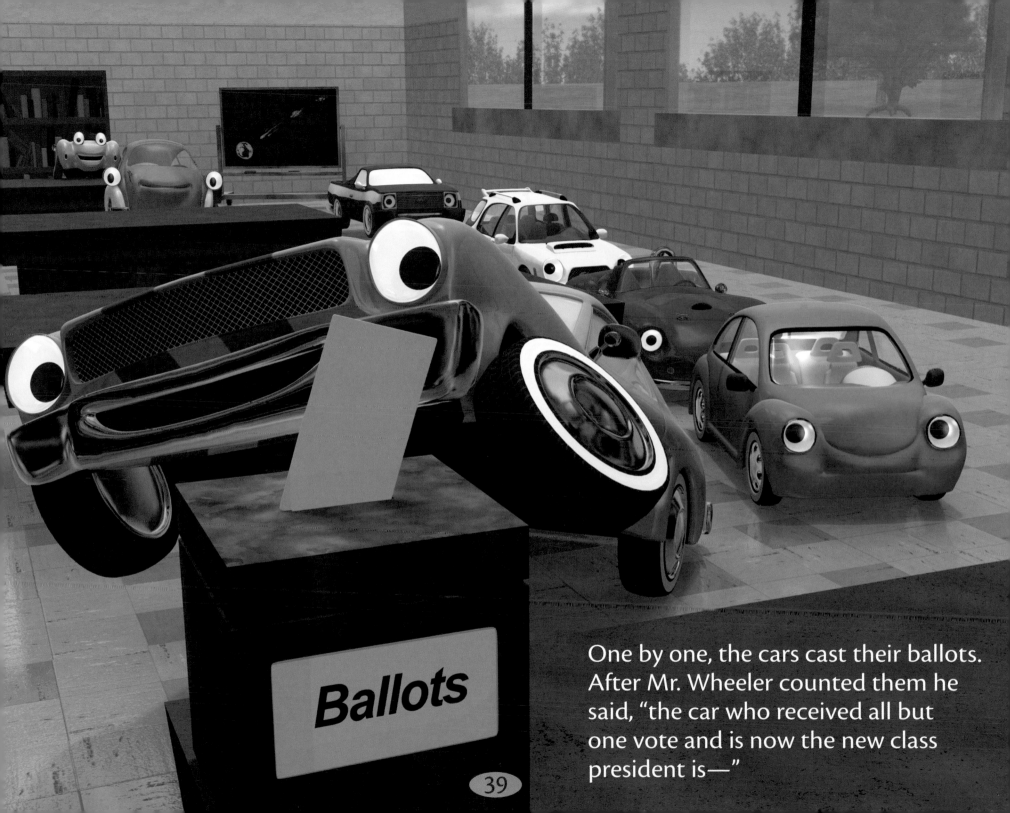

Ballots

One by one, the cars cast their ballots. After Mr. Wheeler counted them he said, "the car who received all but one vote and is now the new class president is—"

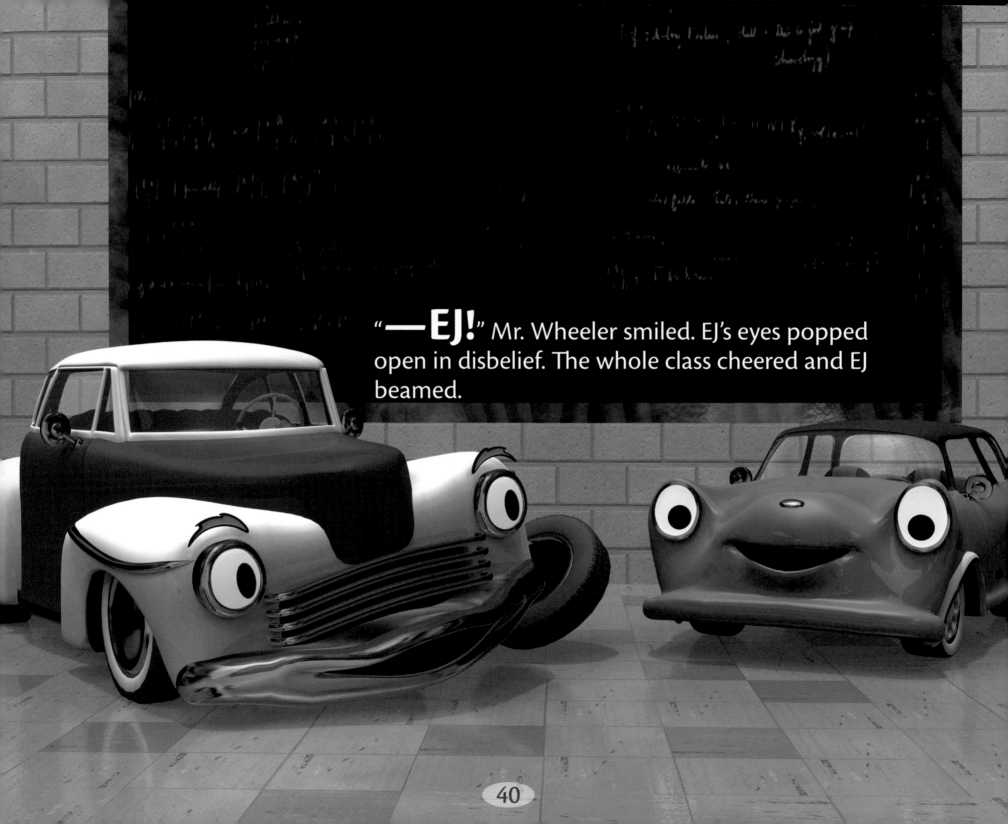

"**—EJ!**" Mr. Wheeler smiled. EJ's eyes popped open in disbelief. The whole class cheered and EJ beamed.

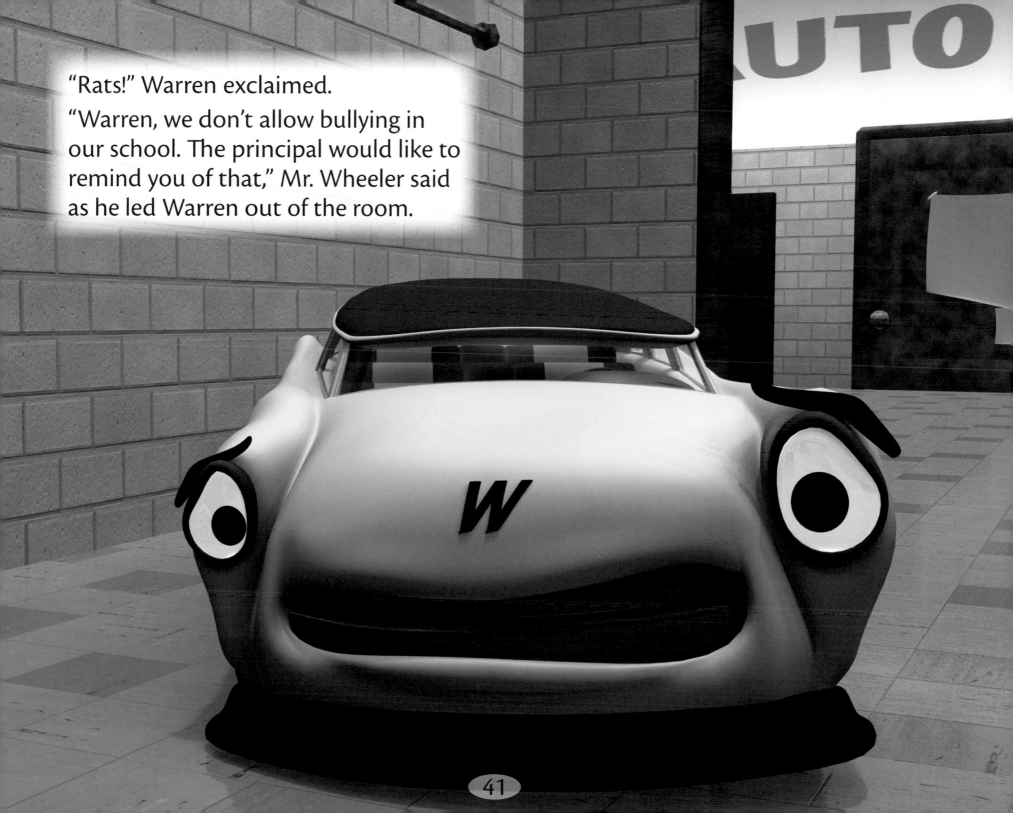

Soon Mr. Wheeler returned and gathered all the cars around him. "EJ, you were very brave today to stand up for yourself like you did."

"Class, I think we should all congratulate EJ," Mr. Wheeler said.

All the kids smiled. "Congratulations, Mr. Class President!"

43

"Thanks, everybody!" EJ said. He felt better than he had in a very long time.

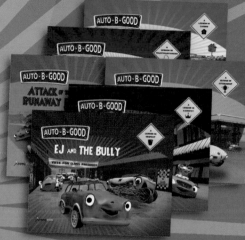